A Thorny P

Volume 0:

Georg Ebers

(Translator: Clara Bell)

Alpha Editions

This edition published in 2023

ISBN : 9789357944434

Design and Setting By
Alpha Editions
www.alphaedis.com
Email - info@alphaedis.com

Contents

VOLUME 1.

CHAPTER I.

The green screen slowly rose, covering the lower portion of the broad studio window where Heron, the gem-cutter, was at work. It was Melissa, the artist's daughter, who had pulled it up, with bended knees and outstretched arms, panting for breath.

"That is enough!" cried her father's impatient voice. He glanced up at the flood of light which the blinding sun of Alexandria was pouring into the room, as it did every autumn afternoon; but as soon as the shadow fell on his work-table the old man's busy fingers were at work again, and he heeded his daughter no more.

An hour later Melissa again, and without any bidding, pulled up the screen as before, but it was so much too heavy for her that the effort brought the blood into her calm, fair face, as the deep, rough "That is enough" was again heard from the work-table.

Then silence reigned once more. Only the artist's low whistling as he worked, or the patter and pipe of the birds in their cages by the window, broke the stillness of the spacious room, till the voice and step of a man were presently heard in the anteroom.

Heron laid by his graver and Melissa her gold embroidery, and the eyes of father and daughter met for the first time for some hours. The very birds seemed excited, and a starling, which had sat moping since the screen had shut the sun out, now cried out, "Olympias!" Melissa rose, and after a swift glance round the room she went to the door, come who might.

Ay, even if the brother she was expecting should bring a companion, or a patron of art who desired her father's work, the room need not fear a critical eye; and she was so well assured of the faultless neatness of her own person, that she only passed a hand over her brown hair, and with an involuntary movement pulled her simple white robe more tightly through her girdle.

Heron's studio was as clean and as simple as his daughter's attire, though it seemed larger than enough for the purpose it served, for only a very small part of it was occupied by the artist, who sat as if in exile behind the work-table on which his belongings were laid out: a set of small instruments in a case, a tray filled with shells and bits of onyx and other agates, a yellow ball of Cyrenian modeling-wax, pumice-stone, bottles, boxes, and bowls.

Melissa had no sooner crossed the threshold, than the sculptor drew up his broad shoulders and brawny person, and raised his hand to fling away the slender stylus he had been using; however, he thought better of it, and laid it carefully aside with the other tools. But this act of self-control must have cost the hot-headed, powerful man a great effort; for he shot a fierce look at the instrument which had had so narrow an escape, and gave it a push of vexation with the back of his hand.

Then he turned towards the door, his sunburnt face looking surly enough, in its frame of tangled gray hair and beard; and, as he waited for the visitor whom Melissa was greeting outside, he tossed back his big head, and threw out his broad, deep chest, as though preparing to wrestle.

Melissa presently returned, and the youth whose hand she still held was, as might be seen in every feature, none other than the sculptor's son. Both were dark-eyed, with noble and splendid heads, and in stature perfectly equal; but while the son's countenance beamed with hearty enjoyment, and seemed by its peculiar attractiveness to be made—and to be accustomed—to charm men and women alike, his father's face was expressive of disgust and misanthropy. It seemed, indeed, as though the newcomer had roused his ire, for Heron answered his son's cheerful greeting with no word but a reproachful "At last!" and paid no heed to the hand the youth held out to him.

Alexander was no doubt inured to such a reception; he did not disturb himself about the old man's ill-humor, but slapped him on the shoulder with rough geniality, went up to the work-table with easy composure, took up the vice which held the nearly finished gem, and, after holding it to the light and examining it carefully, exclaimed: "Well done, father! You have done nothing better than that for a long time."

"Poor stuff!" said his father. But his son laughed.

"If you will have it so. But I will give one of my eyes to see the man in Alexandria who can do the like!"

At this the old man broke out, and shaking his fist he cried: "Because the man who can find anything worth doing, takes good care not to waste his time here, making divine art a mere mockery by such trifling with toys! By Sirius! I should like to fling all those pebbles into the fire, the onyx and shells and jasper and what not, and smash all those wretched tools with these fists, which were certainly made for other work than this."

The youth laid an arm round his father's stalwart neck, and gayly interrupted his wrath. "Oh yes, Father Heron, Philip and I have felt often enough that they know how to hit hard."

"Not nearly often enough," growled the artist, and the young man went on:

"That I grant, though every blow from you was equal to a dozen from the hand of any other father in Alexandria. But that those mighty fists on human arms should have evoked the bewitching smile on the sweet lips of this Psyche, if it is not a miracle of art, is—"

"The degradation of art," the old man put in; but Alexander hastily added:

"The victory of the exquisite over the coarse."

"A victory!" exclaimed Heron, with a scornful flourish of his hand. "I know, boy, why you are trying to garland the oppressive yoke with flowers of flattery. So long as your surly old father sits over the vice, he only whistles a song and spares you his complaints. And then, there is the money his work brings in!"

He laughed bitterly, and as Melissa looked anxiously up at him, her brother exclaimed:

"If I did not know you well, master, and if it would not be too great a pity, I would throw that lovely Psyche to the ostrich in Scopas's court-yard; for, by Herakles! he would swallow your gem more easily than we can swallow such cruel taunts. We do indeed bless the Muses that work brings you some surcease of gloomy thoughts. But for the rest—I hate to speak the word gold. We want it no more than you, who, when the coffer is full, bury it or hide it with the rest. Apollodorus forced a whole talent of the yellow curse upon me for painting his men's room. The sailor's cap, into which I tossed it with the rest, will burst when Seleukus pays me for the portrait of his daughter; and if a thief robs you, and me too, we need not fret over it. My brush and your stylus will earn us more in no time. And what are our needs? We do not bet on quail-fights; we do not run races; I always had a loathing for purchased love; we do not want to wear a heap of garments bought merely because they take our fancy—indeed, I am too hot as it is under this scorching sun. The house is your own. The rent paid by Glaukias, for the work-room and garden you inherited from your father, pays for half at least of what we and the birds and the slaves eat. As for Philip, he lives on air and philosophy; and, besides, he is fed out of the great breadbasket of the Museum."

At this point the starling interrupted the youth's vehement speech with the appropriate cry, "My strength! my strength!" The brother and sister looked at each other, and Alexander went on with genuine enthusiasm:

"But it is not in you to believe us capable of such meanness. Dedicate your next finished work to Isis or Serapis. Let your masterpiece grace the goddess's head-gear, or the god's robe. We shall be quite content, and perhaps the immortals may restore your joy in life as a reward."

The bird repeated its lamentable cry, "My strength!" and the youth proceeded with increased vehemence:

"It would really be better that you should throw your vice and your graver and your burnisher, and all that heap of dainty tools, into the sea, and carve an Atlas such as we have heard you talk about ever since we could first speak

Greek. Come, set to work on a colossus! You have but to speak the word, and the finest clay shall be ready on your modeling-table by to-morrow, either here or in Glaukias's work-room, which is indeed your own. I know where the best is to be found, and can bring it to you in any quantity. Scopas will lend me his wagon. I can see it now, and you valiantly struggling with it till your mighty arms ache. You will not whistle and hum over that, but sing out with all your might, as you used when my mother was alive, when you and your apprentices joined Dionysus's drunken rout. Then your brow will grow smooth again; and if the model is a success, and you want to buy marble, or pay the founder, then out with your gold, out of the coffer and its hiding-place! Then you can make use of all your strength, and your dream of producing an Atlas such as the world has not seen—your beautiful dream—will become a reality!"

Heron had listened eagerly to his son's rhapsody, but he now cast a timid glance at the table where the wax and tools lay, pushed the rough hair from his brow, and broke in with a bitter laugh: "My dream, do you say— my dream? As if I did not know too well that I am no longer the man to create an Atlas! As if I did not feel, without your words, that my strength for it is a thing of the past!"

"Nay, father," exclaimed the painter. "Is it right to cast away the sword before the battle? And even if you did not succeed—"

"You would be all the better pleased," the sculptor put in. "What surer way could there be to teach the old simpleton, once for all, that the time when he could do great work is over and gone?"

"That is unjust, father; that is unworthy of you," the young man interrupted in great excitement; but his father went on, raising his voice; "Silence, boy! One thing at any rate is left to me, as you know— my keen eyes; and they did not fail me when you two looked at each other as the starling cried, 'My strength!' Ay, the bird is in the right when he bewails what was once so great and is now a mere laughing-stock. But you—you ought to reverence the man to whom you owe your existence and all you know; you allow yourself to shrug your shoulders over your own father's humbler art, since your first pictures were fairly successful. —How puffed up he is, since, by my devoted care, he has been a painter! How he looks down on the poor wretch who, by the pinch of necessity, has come down from being a sculptor of the highest promise to being a mere gem-cutter! In the depths of your soul—and I know it—you regard my laborious art as half a handicraft. Well, perhaps it deserves no better name; but that you—both of you—should make common cause with a bird, and mock the sacred fire which still burns in an old man, and moves him to serve true and noble art and to mold something great—an Atlas such as the world has never seen on a heroic scale; that—"

He covered his face with his hands and sobbed aloud. And the strong man's passionate grief cut his children to the heart, though, since their mother's death, their father's rage and discontent had many a time ere now broken down into childish lamentation.

To-day no doubt the old man was in worse spirits than usual, for it was the day of the Nekysia—the feast of the dead kept every autumn; and he had that morning visited his wife's grave, accompanied by his daughter, and had anointed the tombstone and decked it with flowers. The young people tried to comfort him; and when at last he was more composed and had dried his tears, he said, in so melancholy and subdued a tone that the angry blusterer was scarcely recognizable: "There—leave me alone; it will soon be over. I will finish this gem to-morrow, and then I must do the Serapis I promised Theophilus, the high-priest. Nothing can come of the Atlas. Perhaps you meant it in all sincerity, Alexander; but since your mother left me, children, since then—my arms are no weaker than they were; but in here—what it was that shriveled, broke, leaked away—I can not find words for it. If you care for me—and I know you do—you must not be vexed with me if my gall rises now and then; there is too much bitterness in my soul. I can not reach the goal I strive after and was meant to win; I have lost what I loved best, and where am I to find comfort or compensation?"

His children tenderly assured him of their affection, and he allowed Melissa to kiss him, and stroked Alexander's hair.

Then he inquired for Philip, his eldest son and his favorite; and on learning that he, the only person who, as he believed, could understand him, would not come to see him this day above all others, he again broke out in wrath, abusing the degeneracy of the age and the ingratitude of the young.

"Is it a visit which detains him again?" he inquired, and when Alexander thought not, he exclaimed contemptuously: "Then it is some war of words at the Museum. And for such poor stuff as that a son can forget his duty to his father and mother!"

"But you, too, used to enjoy these conflicts of intellect," his daughter humbly remarked; but the old man broke in:

"Only because they help a miserable world to forget the torments of existence, and the hideous certainty of having been born only to die some horrible death. But what can you know of this?"

"By my mother's death-bed," replied the girl, "we, too, had a glimpse into the terrible mystery." And Alexander gravely added, "And since we last met, father, I may certainly account myself as one of the initiated."

"You have painted a dead body?" asked his father.

"Yes, father," replied the lad with a deep breath. "I warned you," said Heron, in a tone of superior experience.

And then, as Melissa rearranged the folds of his blue robe, he said he should go for a walk. He sighed as he spoke, and his children knew whither he would go. It was to the grave to which Melissa had accompanied him that morning; and he would visit it alone, to meditate undisturbed on the wife he had lost.

CHAPTER II.

The brother and sister were left together. Melissa sighed deeply; but her brother went up to her, laid his arm round her shoulder, and said: "Poor child! you have indeed a hard time of it. Eighteen years old, and as pretty as you are, to be kept locked up as if in prison! No one would envy you, even if your fellow-captive and keeper were younger and less gloomy than your father is! But we know what it all means. His grief eats into his soul, and it does him as much good to storm and scold, as it does us to laugh."

"If only the world could know how kind his heart really is!" said the girl.

"He is not the same to his friends as to us," said Alexander; but Melissa shook her head, and said sadly: "He broke out yesterday against Apion, the dealer, and it was dreadful. For the fiftieth time he had waited supper for you two in vain, and in the twilight, when he had done work, his grief overcame him, and to see him weep is quite heartbreaking! The Syrian dealer came in and found him all tearful, and being so bold as to jest about it in his flippant way—"

"The old man would give him his answer, I know!" cried her brother with a hearty laugh. "He will not again be in a hurry to stir up a wounded lion."

"That is the very word," said Melissa, and her large eyes sparkled. "At the fight in the Circus, I could not help thinking of my father, when the huge king of the desert lay with a broken spear in his loins, whining loudly, and burying his maned head between his great paws. The gods are pitiless!"

"Indeed they are," replied the youth, with deep conviction; but his sister looked up at him in surprise.

"Do you say so, Alexander? Yes, indeed—you looked just now as I never saw you before. Has misfortune overtaken you too?"

"Misfortune?" he repeated, and he gently stroked her hair. "No, not exactly; and you know my woes sit lightly enough on me. The immortals have indeed shown me very plainly that it is their will sometimes to spoil the feast of life with a right bitter draught. But, like the moon itself, all it shines on is doomed to change—happily! Many things here below seem strangely ordered. Like ears and eyes, hands and feet, many things are by nature double, and misfortunes, as they say, commonly come in couples yoked like oxen."

"Then you have had some twofold blow?" asked Melissa, clasping her hands over her anxiously throbbing bosom.

"I, child! No, indeed. Nothing has befallen your father's younger son; and if I were a philosopher, like Philip, I should be moved to wonder why a man can only be wet when the rain falls on him, and yet can be so wretched when disaster falls on another. But do not look at me with such terror in your great eyes. I swear to you that, as a man and an artist, I never felt better, and so I ought properly to be in my usual frame of mind. But the skeleton at life's festival has been shown to me. What sort of thing is that? It is an image— the image of a dead man which was carried round by the Egyptians, and is to this day by the Romans, to remind the feasters that they should fill every hour with enjoyment, since enjoyment is all too soon at an end. Such an image, child—"

"You are thinking of the dead girl—Seleukus's daughter—whose portrait you are painting?" asked Melissa.

Alexander nodded, sat down on the bench by his sister, and, taking up her needlework, exclaimed "Give us some light, child. I want to see your pretty face. I want to be sure that Diodorus did not perjure himself when, at the 'Crane,' the other day, he swore that it had not its match in Alexandria. Besides, I hate the darkness."

When Melissa returned with the lighted lamp, she found her brother, who was not wont to keep still, sitting in the place where she had left him. But he sprang up as she entered, and prevented her further greeting by exclaiming:

"Patience! patience! You shall be told all. Only I did not want to worry you on the day of the festival of the dead. And besides, to-morrow perhaps he will be in a better frame of mind, and next day—"

Melissa became urgent. "If Philip is ill—" she put in.

"Not exactly ill," said he. "He has no fever, no ague-fit, no aches and pains. He is not in bed, and has no bitter draughts to swallow. Yet is he not well, any more than I, though but just now, in the dining-hall at the Elephant, I ate like a starving wolf, and could at this moment jump over this table. Shall I prove it?"

"No, no," said his sister, in growing distress. "But, if you love me, tell me at once and plainly—"At once and plainly," sighed the painter. "That, in any case, will not be easy. But I will do my best. You knew Korinna?"

"Seleukus's daughter?"

"She herself—the maiden from whose corpse I am painting her portrait."

"No. But you wanted—"

"I wanted to be brief, but I care even more to be understood; and if you have never seen with your own eyes, if you do not yourself know what a miracle of beauty the gods wrought when they molded that maiden, you are indeed justified in regarding me as a fool and Philip as a madman—which, thank the gods, he certainly is not yet."

"Then he too has seen the dead maiden?"

"No, no. And yet—perhaps. That at present remains a mystery. I hardly know what happened even to myself. I succeeded in controlling myself in my father's presence; but now, when it all rises up before me, before my very eyes, so distinct, so real, so tangible, now—by Sirius! Melissa, if you interrupt me again—"

"Begin again. I will be silent," she cried. "I can easily picture your Korinna as a divinely beautiful creature."

Alexander raised his hands to heaven, exclaiming with passionate vehemence: "Oh, how would I praise and glorify the gods, who formed that marvel of their art, and my mouth should be full of their grace and mercy, if they had but allowed the world to sun itself in the charm of that glorious creature, and to worship their everlasting beauty in her who was their image! But they have wantonly destroyed their own masterpiece, have crushed the scarce-opened bud, have darkened the star ere it has risen! If a man had done it, Melissa, a man what would his doom have been! If he—"

Here the youth hid his face in his hands in passionate emotion; but, feeling his sister's arm round his shoulder, he recovered himself, and went on more calmly: "Well, you heard that she was dead. She was of just your age; she is dead at eighteen, and her father commissioned me to paint her in death.— Pour me out some water; then I will proceed as coldly as a man crying the description of a runaway slave." He drank a deep draught, and wandered restlessly up and down in front of his sister, while he told her all that had happened to him during the last few days.

The day before yesterday, at noon, he had left the inn where he had been carousing with friends, gay and careless, and had obeyed the call of Seleukus. Just before raising the knocker he had been singing cheerfully to himself. Never had he felt more fully content—the gayest of the gay. One of the first men in the town, and a connoisseur, had honored him with a fine commission, and the prospect of painting something dead had pleased him. His old master had often admired the exquisite delicacy of the flesh-tones of a recently deceased body. As his glance fell on the implements that his slave carried after him, he had drawn himself up with the proud feeling of having before him a noble task, to which he felt equal. Then the porter, a gray-bearded Gaul, had opened the door to him, and as he looked into his care-worn face and received from him a silent permission to step in, he had already become more serious.

He had heard marvels of the magnificence of the house that he now entered; and the lofty vestibule into which he was admitted, the mosaic floor that he trod; the marble statues and high reliefs round the upper hart of the walls, were well worth careful observation; yet he, whose eyes usually carried away so vivid an impression of what he had once seen that he could draw it from memory, gave no attention to any particular thing among the various objects worthy of admiration. For already in the anteroom a peculiar sensation had come over him. The large halls, which were filled with odors of ambergris and incense, were as still as the grave. And it seemed to him that even the sun, which had been shining brilliantly a few minutes before in a cloudless sky, had disappeared behind clouds, for a strange twilight, unlike anything he had ever seen, surrounded him. Then he perceived that it came in through the black velarium with which they had closed the open roof of the room through which he was passing.

In the anteroom a young freedman had hurried silently past him—had vanished like a shadow through the dusky rooms. His duty must have been to announce the artist's arrival to the mother of the dead girl; for, before Alexander had found time to feast his gaze on the luxurious mass of flowering plants that surrounded the fountain in the middle of the impluvium, a tall matron, in flowing mourning garments, came towards him —Korinna's mother.

Without lifting the black veil which enveloped her from head to foot, she speechlessly signed him to follow her. Till this moment not even a whisper had met his ear from any human lips in this house of death and mourning; and the stillness was so oppressive to the light-hearted young painter, that, merely to hear the sound of his own voice, he ex-plained to the lady who he was and wherefore he had come. But the only answer was a dumb assenting bow of the head.

He had not far to go with his stately guide; their walk ended in a spacious room. It had been made a perfect flower-garden with hundreds of magnificent plants; piles of garlands strewed the floor, and in the midst stood the couch on which lay the dead girl. In this hall, too, reigned the same gloomy twilight which had startled him in the vestibule.

The dim, shrouded form lying motionless on the couch before him, with a heavy wreath of lotus-flowers and white roses encircling it from head to foot, was the subject for his brush. He was to paint here, where he could scarcely distinguish one plant from another, or make out the form of the vases which stood round the bed of death. The white blossoms alone gleamed like pale lights in the gloom, and with a sister radiance something smooth and round which lay on the couch—the bare arm of the dead maiden.

His heart began to throb; the artist's love of his art had awaked within him; he had collected his wits, and explained to the matron that to paint in the darkness was impossible.

Again she bowed in reply, but at a signal two waiting women, who were squatting on the floor behind the couch, started up in the twilight, as if they had sprung from the earth, and approached their mistress.

A fresh shock chilled the painter's blood, for at the same moment the lady's voice was suddenly audible close to his ear, almost as deep as a man's but not unmelodious, ordering the girls to draw back the curtain as far as the painter should desire.

Now, he felt, the spell was broken; curiosity and eagerness took the place of reverence for death. He quietly gave his orders for the necessary arrangements, lent the women the help of his stronger arm, took out his painting implements, and then requested the matron to unveil the dead girl, that he might see from which side it would be best to take the portrait. But then again he was near losing his composure, for the lady raised her veil, and measured him with a glance as though he had asked something strange and audacious indeed.

Never had he met so piercing a glance from any woman's eyes; and yet they were red with weeping and full of tears. Bitter grief spoke in every line of her still youthful features, and their stern, majestic beauty was in keeping with the deep tones of her speech. Oh that he had been so happy as to see this woman in the bloom of youthful loveliness! She did not heed his admiring surprise; before acceding to his demand, her regal form trembled from head to foot, and she sighed as she lifted the shroud from her daughter's face. Then, with a groan, she dropped on her knees by the couch and laid her cheek against that of the dead maiden. At last she rose, and murmured to the painter that if he were successful in his task her gratitude would be beyond expression.

"What more she said," Alexander went on, "I could but half understand, for she wept all the time, and I could not collect my thoughts. It was not till afterward that I learned from her waiting-woman—a Christian— that she meant to tell me that the relations and wailing women were to come to-morrow morning. I could paint on till nightfall, but no longer. I had been chosen for the task because Seleukus had heard from my old teacher, Bion, that I should get a faithful likeness of the original more quickly than any one else. She may have said more, but I heard nothing; I only saw. For when the veil no longer hid that face from my gaze, I felt as though the gods had revealed a mystery to me which till now only the immortals had been permitted to know. Never was my soul so steeped in devotion, never had my heart beat in such solemn uplifting as at that moment. What I was gazing at and had to represent was a thing neither human nor divine; it was beauty itself—that beauty of which I have often dreamed in blissful rapture.

"And yet—do not misapprehend me—I never thought of bewailing the maiden, or grieving over her early death. She was but sleeping—I could fancy: I watched one I loved in her slumbers. My heart beat high! Ay, child, and the work I did was pure joy, such joy as only the gods on Olympus know at their golden board. Every feature, every line was of such perfection as only the artist's soul can conceive of, nay, even dream of. The ecstasy remained, but my unrest gave way to an indescribable and wordless bliss. I drew with the red chalk, and mixed the colors with the grinder, and all the while I could not feel the painful sense of painting a corpse. If she were slumbering, she had fallen asleep with bright images in her memory. I even fancied again and again that her lips moved her exquisitely chiseled mouth, and that a faint breath played with her abundant, waving, shining brown hair, as it does with yours.

"The Muse sped my hand and the portrait—Bion and the rest will praise it, I think, though it is no more like the unapproachable original than that lamp is like the evening star yonder."

"And shall we be allowed to see it?" asked Melissa, who had been listening breathlessly to her brother's narrative.

The words seemed to have snatched the artist from a dream. He had to pause and consider where he was and to whom he was speaking. He hastily pushed the curling hair off his damp brow, and said:

"I do not understand. What is it you ask?"

"I only asked whether we should be allowed to see the portrait," she answered timidly. "I was wrong to interrupt you. But how hot your head is! Drink again before you go on. Had you really finished by sundown?"

Alexander shook his head, drank, and then went on more calmly: "No, no! It is a pity you spoke. In fancy I was painting her still. There is the moon rising already. I must make haste. I have told you all this for Philip's sake, not for my own."

"I will not interrupt you again, I assure you," said Melissa. "Well, well," said her brother. "There is not much that is pleasant left to tell. Where was I?"

"Painting, so long as it was light—"

"To be sure—I remember. It began to grow dark. Then lamps were brought in, large ones, and as many as I wished for. Just before sunset Seleukus, Korinna's father, came in to look upon his daughter once more. He bore his grief with dignified composure; yet by his child's bier he found it hard to be calm. But you can imagine all that. He invited me to eat, and the food they brought might have tempted a full man to excess, but I could only swallow a few mouthfuls. Berenike—the mother—did not even moisten her lips, but Seleukus did duty for us both, and this I could see displeased his wife. During supper the merchant made many inquiries about me and my father; for he had heard Philip's praises from his brother Theophilus, the high-priest. I learned from him that Korinna had caught her sickness from a slave girl she had nursed, and had died of the fever in three days. But while I sat listening to him, as he talked and ate, I could not keep my eyes off his wife who reclined opposite to me silent and motionless, for the gods had created Korinna in her very image. The lady Berenike's eyes indeed sparkle with a lurid, I might almost say an alarming, fire, but they are shaped like Korinna's. I said so, and asked whether they were of the same color; I wanted to know for my portrait. On this Seleukus referred me to a picture painted by old Sosibius, who has lately gone to Rome to work in Caesar's new baths. He last year painted the wall of a room in the mer chant's country house at Kanopus. In the center of the picture stands Galatea, and I know it now to be a good and true likeness.

"The picture I finished that evening is to be placed at the head of the young girl's sarcophagus; but I am to keep it two days longer, to reproduce a second likeness more at my leisure, with the help of the Galatea, which is to remain in Seleukus's town house.

"Then he left me alone with his wife.

"What a delightful commission! I set to work with renewed pleasure, and more composure than at first. I had no need to hurry, for the first picture is to be hidden in the tomb, and I could give all my care to the second. Besides, Korinna's features were indelibly impressed on my eye.

"I generally can not paint at all by lamp-light; but this time I found no difficulty, and I soon recovered that blissful, solemn mood which I had felt in the presence of the dead. Only now and then it was clouded by a sigh, or a faint moan from Berenike: 'Gone, gone! There is no comfort— none, none!'

"And what could I answer? When did Death ever give back what he has snatched away?

"' I can not even picture her as she was,' she murmured sadly to herself — but this I might remedy by the help of my art, so I painted on with increasing zeal; and at last her lamentations ceased to trouble me, for she fell asleep, and her handsome head sank on her breast. The watchers, too, had dropped asleep, and only their deep breathing broke the stillness.

"Suddenly it flashed upon me that I was alone with Korinna, and the feeling grew stronger and stronger; I fancied her lovely lips had moved, that a smile gently parted them, inviting me to kiss them. As often as I looked at them—and they bewitched me—I saw and felt the same, and at last every impulse within me drove me toward her, and I could no longer resist: my lips pressed hers in a kiss!"

Melissa softly sighed, but the artist did not hear; he went on: "And in that kiss I became hers; she took the heart and soul of me. I can no longer escape from her; awake or asleep, her image is before my eyes, and my spirit is in her power."

Again he drank, emptying the cup at one deep gulp. Then he went on: "So be it! Who sees a god, they say, must die. And it is well, for he has known something more glorious than other men. Our brother Philip, too, lives with his heart in bonds to that one alone, unless a demon has cheated his senses. I am troubled about him, and you must help me."

He sprang up, pacing the room again with long strides, but his sister clung to his arm and besought him to shake off the bewitching vision. How earnest was her prayer, what eager tenderness rang in her every word, as she entreated him to tell her when and where her elder brother, too, had met the daughter of Seleukus!

The artist's soft heart was easily moved. Stroking the hair of the loving creature at his side—so helpful as a rule, but now bewildered —he tried to calm her by affecting a lighter mood than he really felt, assuring her that he should soon recover his usual good spirits. She knew full well, he said, that his living loves changed in frequent succession, and it would be strange indeed if a dead one could bind him any longer. And his adventure, so far as it concerned the house of Seleukus, ended with that kiss; for the lady Berenike had presently waked, and urged him to finish the portrait at his own house.

Next morning he had completed it with the help of the Galatea in the villa at Kanopus, and he had heard a great deal about the dead maiden. A young woman who was left in charge of the villa had supplied him with whatever he needed. Her pretty face was swollen with weeping, and it was in a voice choked with tears that she had told him that her husband, who was a centurion in Caesar's pretorian guard, would arrive to-morrow or next day at Alexandria, with his imperial master. She had not seen him for a long time, and had an infant to show him which he had not yet seen; and yet she could not be glad, for her young mistress's death had extinguished all her joy.

"The affection which breathed in every word of the centurion's wife," Alexander said, "helped me in my work. I could be satisfied with the result.

"The picture is so successful that I finished that for Seleukus in all confidence, and for the sarcophagus I will copy it as well or as ill as time will allow. It will hardly be seen in the half-dark tomb, and how few will ever go to see it! None but a Seleukus can afford to employ so costly a brush as your brother's is—thank the Muses! But the second portrait is quite another thing, for that may chance to be hung next a picture by Apelles; and it must restore to the parents so much of their lost child as it lies in my power to give them. So, on my way, I made up my mind to begin the copy at once by lamp-light, for it must be ready by to-morrow night at latest.

"I hurried to my work-room, and my slave placed the picture on an easel, while I welcomed my brother Philip who had come to see me, and who had lighted a lamp, and of course had brought a book. He was so absorbed in it that he did not observe that I had come in till I addressed him. Then I told him whence I came and what had happened, and he thought it all very strange and interesting.

"He was as usual rather hurried and hesitating, not quite clear, but understanding it all. Then he began telling me something about a philosopher who has just come to the front, a porter by trade, from whom he had heard sundry wonders, and it was not till Syrus brought me in a supper of oysters— for I could still eat nothing more solid—that he asked to see the portrait.

"I pointed to the easel, and watched him; for the harder he is to please, the more I value his opinion. This time I felt confident of praise, or even of some admiration, if only for the beauty of the model.

"He threw off the veil from the picture with a hasty movement, but, instead of gazing at it calmly, as he is wont, and snapping out his sharp criticisms, he staggered backward, as though the noonday sun had dazzled his sight. Then, bending forward, he stared at the painting, panting as he might after racing for a wager. He stood in perfect silence, for I know not how long, as though it were Medusa he was gazing on, and when at last he clasped his hand to his brow, I called him by name. He made no reply, but an impatient 'Leave me alone!' and then he still gazed at the face as though to devour it with his eyes, and without a sound.

"I did not disturb him; for, thought I, he too is bewitched by the exquisite beauty of those virgin features. So we were both silent, till he asked, in a choked voice: 'And did you paint that? Is that, do you say, the daughter that Seleukus has just lost?'

"Of course I said 'Yes'; but then he turned on me in a rage, and reproached me bitterly for deceiving and cheating him, and jesting with things that to him were sacred, though I might think them a subject for sport.

"I assured him that my answer was as earnest as it was accurate, and that every word of my story was true.

"This only made him more furious. I, too, began to get angry, and as he, evidently deeply agitated, still persisted in saying that my picture could not have been painted from the dead Korinna, I swore to him solemnly, with the most sacred oath I could think of, that it was really so.

"On this he declared to me in words so tender and touching as I never before heard from his lips, that if I were deceiving him his peace of mind would be forever destroyed-nay, that he feared for his reason; and when I had repeatedly assured him, by the memory of our departed mother, that I had never dreamed of playing a trick upon him, he shook his head, grasped his brow, and turned to leave the room without another word."

"And you let him go?" cried Melissa, in anxious alarm.

"Certainly not," replied the painter. "On the contrary, I stood in his way, and asked him whether he had known Korinna, and what all this might mean. But he would make no reply, and tried to pass me and get away. It must have been a strange scene, for we two big men struggled as if we were at a wrestling-match. I got him down with one hand behind his knees, and so he had to remain; and when I had promised to let him go, he confessed that he had seen Korinna at the house of her uncle, the high- priest, without knowing who she was or even speaking a word to her. And he, who usually flees from every creature wearing a woman's robe, had never forgotten that maiden and her noble beauty; and, though he did not say so, it was obvious, from every word, that he was madly in love. Her eyes had followed him wherever he went, and this he deemed a great misfortune, for it had disturbed his power of thought. A month since he went across Lake Mareotis to Polybius to visit Andreas, and while, on his return, he was standing on the shore, he saw her again, with an old man in white robes. But the last time he saw her was on the morning of the very day when all this happened; and if he is to be believed, he not only saw her but touched her hand. That, again, was by the lake; she was just stepping out of the ferry-boat. The obolus she had ready to pay the oarsman dropped on the ground, and Philip picked it up and returned it to her. Then his fingers touched hers. He could feel it still, he declared, and yet she had then ceased to walk among the living.

"Then it was my turn to doubt his word; but he maintained that his story was true in every detail; he would hear nothing said about some one resembling her, or anything of the kind, and spoke of daimons showing him false visions, to cheat him and hinder him from working out his investigations of the real nature of things to a successful issue. But this is in direct antagonism to his views of daimons; and when at last he rushed out of the house, he looked like one possessed of evil spirits.

"I hurried after him, but he disappeared down a dark alley. Then I had enough to do to finish my copy, and yesterday I carried it home to Seleukus.

"Then I had time to look for Philip, but I could hear nothing of him, either in his own lodgings or at the Museum. To-day I have been hunting for him since early in the morning. I even forgot to lay any flowers on my mother's grave, as usual on the day of the Nekysia, because I was thinking only of him. But he no doubt is gone to the city of the dead; for, on my way hither, as I was ordering a garland in the flower-market, pretty little Doxion showed me two beauties which she had woven for him, and which he is presently to fetch. So he must now be in the Nekropolis; and I know for whom he intends the second; for the door-keeper at Seleukus's house told me that a man, who said he was my brother, had twice called, and had eagerly inquired whether my picture had yet been attached to Korinna's sarcophagus. The old man told him it had not, because, of course, the embalming could not be complete as yet. But the picture was to be displayed to-day, as being the feast of the dead, in the hall of the embalmers. That was the plan, I know. So, now, child, set your wise little woman's head to work, and devise something by which he may be brought to his senses, and released from these crazy imaginings."

"The first thing to be done," Melissa exclaimed, "is to follow him and talk to him.-Wait a moment; I must speak a word to the slaves. My father's night-draught can be mixed in a minute. He might perhaps return home before us, and I must leave his couch—I will be with you in a minute."

CHAPTER III.

The brother and sister had walked some distance. The roads were full of people, and the nearer they came to the Nekropolis the denser was the throng.

As they skirted the town walls they took counsel together.

Being perfectly agreed that the girl who had touched Philip's hand could certainly be no daimon who had assumed Korinna's form, they were inclined to accept the view that a strong resemblance had deceived their brother. They finally decided that Alexander should try to discover the maiden who so strangely resembled the dead; and the artist was ready for the task, for he could only work when his heart was light, and had never felt such a weight on it before. The hope of meeting with a living creature who resembled that fair dead maiden, combined with his wish to rescue his brother from the disorder of mind which threatened him; and Melissa perceived with glad surprise how quickly this new object in life restored the youth's happy temper.

It was she who spoke most, and Alexander, whom nothing escaped that had any form of beauty, feasted his ear on the pearly ring of her voice.

"And her face is to match," thought he as they went on in the darkness; "and may the Charites who have endowed her with every charm, forgive my father for burying her as he does his gold."

It was not in his nature to keep anything that stirred him deeply to himself, when he was in the society of another, so he murmured to his sister: "It is just as well that the Macedonian youths of this city should not be able to see what a jewel our old man's house contains. —Look how brightly Selene shines on us, and how gloriously the stars burn! Nowhere do the heavens blaze more brilliantly than here. As soon as we come out of the shadow that the great walls cast on the road we shall be in broad light. There is the Serapeum rising out of the darkness. They are rehearsing the great illumination which is to dazzle the eyes of Caesar when he comes. But they must show too, that to-night, at least, the gods of the nether world and death are all awake. You can never have been in the Nekropolis at so late an hour before."

"How should I?" replied the girl. And he expressed the pleasure that it gave him to be able to show her for the first time the wonderful night scene of such a festival. And when he heard the deep-drawn "Ah!" with which she hailed the sight of the greatest temple of all, blazing in the midst of the darkness with tar-pans, torches, and lamps innumerable, he replied with as much pride and satisfaction as though she owed the display to him, "Ay, what do you think of that?"

Above the huge stone edifice which was thus lighted up, the dome of the Serapeum rose high into the air, its summit appearing to touch the sky. Never had the gigantic structure seemed so beautiful to the girl, who had only seen it by daylight; for under the illumination, arranged by a master-hand, every line stood out more clearly than in the sunlight; and in the presence of this wonderful sight Melissa's impressionable young soul forgot the trouble that had weighed on it, and her heart beat higher.

Her lonely life with her father had hitherto fully satisfied her, and she had, never yet dreamed of anything better in the future than a quiet and modest existence, caring for him and her brothers; but now she thankfully experienced the pleasure of seeing for once something really grand and fine, and rejoiced at having escaped for a while from the monotony of each day and hour.

Once, too, she had been with her brothers and Diodoros, Alexander's greatest friend, to see a wild-beast fight, followed by a combat of gladiators; but she had come home frightened and sorrowful, for what she had seen had horrified more than it had interested her. Some of the killed and tortured beings haunted her mind; and, besides, sitting in the lowest and best seats belonging to Diodoros's wealthy father, she had been stared at so boldly and defiantly whenever she raised her eyes, by a young gallant opposite, that she had felt vexed and insulted; nay, had wished above all things to get home as soon as possible. And yet she had loved Diodoros from her childhood, and she would have enjoyed sitting quietly by his side more than looking on at the show.

But on this occasion her curiosity was gratified, and the hope of being able to help one who was dear to her filled her with quiet gladness. It was a comfort to her, too, to find herself once more by her mother's grave with Alexander, who was her especial friend. She could never come here often enough, and the blessing which emanated from it—of that she was convinced—must surely fall on her brother also, and avert from him all that grieved his heart.

As they walked on between the Serapeum on one hand, towering high above all else, and the Stadium on the other, the throng was dense; on the bridge over the canal it was difficult to make any progress. Now, as the full moon rose, the sacrifices and games in honor of the gods of the under world were beginning, and now the workshops and factories had emptied themselves into the streets already astir for the festival of the dead, so every moment the road became more crowded.

Such a tumult was generally odious to her retiring nature; but to-night she felt herself merely one drop in the great, flowing river, of which every other drop felt the same impulse which was carrying her forward to her destination. The desire to show the dead that they were not forgotten, that their favor was courted and hoped for, animated men and women, old and young alike.

There were few indeed who had not a wreath or a posy in their hands, or carried behind them by a slave. In front of the brother and sister was a large family of children. A black nurse carried the youngest on her shoulder, and an ass bore a basket in which were flowers for the tomb, with a wineflask and eatables. A memorial banquet was to be held at the grave of their ancestors; and the little one, whose golden head rose above the black, woolly poll of the negress, nodded gayly in response to Melissa's smiles. The children were enchanted at the prospect of a meal at such an unusual hour, and their parents rejoiced in them and in the solemn pleasure they anticipated.

Many a one in this night of remembrance only cared to recall the happy hours spent in the society of the beloved dead; others hoped to leave their grief and pain behind them, and find fresh courage and contentment in the City of the Dead; for tonight the gates of the nether world stood open, and now, if ever, the gods that reigned there would accept the offerings and hear the prayers of the devout.

Those lean Egyptians, who pushed past in silence and haranging their heads, were no doubt bent on carrying offerings to Osiris and Anubis—for the festival of the gods of death and resurrection coincided with the Nekysia— and on winning their favors by magical formulas and spells.

Everything was plainly visible, for the desert tract of the Nekropolis, where at this hour utter darkness and silence usually reigned, was brightly lighted up. Still, the blaze failed to banish entirely the thrill of fear which pervaded the spot at night; for the unwonted glare dazzled and bewildered the bats and night-birds, and they fluttered about over the heads of the intruders in dark, ghostly flight. Many a one believed them to be the unresting souls of condemned sinners, and looked up at them with awe.

Melissa drew her veil closer and clung more tightly to her brother, for a sound of singing and wild cries, which she had heard behind her for some time, was now coming closer. They were no longer treading the paved street, but the hard-beaten soil of the desert. The crush was over, for here the crowd could spread abroad; but the uproarious troop, which she did not even dare to look at, came rushing past quite close to them. They were Greeks, of all ages and of both sexes. The men flourished torches, and were shouting a song with unbridled vehemence; the women, wearing garlands, kept up with them. What they carried in the baskets on their heads could not be seen, nor did Alexander know; for so many religious brotherhoods and mystic societies existed here that it was impossible to guess to which this noisy troop might belong.

The pair had presently overtaken a little train of white-robed men moving forward at a solemn pace, whom the painter recognized as the philosophical and religious fraternity of the Neo-Pythagoreans, when a small knot of men and women in the greatest excitement came rushing past as if they were mad. The men wore the loose red caps of their Phrygian land; the women carried bowls full of fruits. Some beat small drums, others clanged cymbals, and each hauled his neighbor along with deafening cries, faster and faster, till the dust hid them from sight and a new din drowned the last, for the votaries of Dionysus were already close upon them, and vied with the Phrygians in uproariousness. But this wild troop remained behind; for one of the light-colored oxen, covered with decorations, which was being driven in the procession by a party of men and boys, to be presently sacrificed, had broken away, maddened by the lights and the shouting, and had to be caught and led again.

At last they reached the graveyard. But even now they could not make their way to the long row of houses where the embalmers dwelt, for an impenetrable mass of human beings stood pent up in front of them, and Melissa begged her brother to give her a moment's breathing space.

All she had seen and heard on the way had excited her greatly; but she had scarcely for a moment forgotten what it was that had brought her out so late, who it was that she sought, or that it would need her utmost endeavor to free him from the delusion that had fooled him. In this dense throng and deafening tumult it was scarcely possible to recover that collected calm which she had found in the morning at her mother's tomb. In that, doubt had had no part, and the delightful feeling of freedom which had shone on her soul, now shrank deep into the shade before a growing curiosity and the longing for her usual repose.

If her father were to find her here! When she saw a tall figure resembling his cross the torchlight, all clouded as it was by the dust, she drew her brother away behind the stall of a seller of drinks and other refreshments. The father, at any rate, must be spared the distress she felt about Philip, who was his favorite. Besides, she knew full well that, if he met her here, he would at once take her home.

The question now was where Philip might be found.

They were standing close to the booths where itinerant dealers sold food and liquors of every description, flowers and wreaths, amulets and papyrus-leaves, with strange charms written on them to secure health for the living and salvation for the souls of the dead. An astrologer, who foretold the course of a man's life from the position of the planets, had erected a high platform with large tables displayed to view, and the instrument wherewith he aimed at the stars as it were with a bow; and his Syrian slave, accompanying himself on a gayly-painted drum, proclaimed his master's powers. There were closed tents in which magical remedies were to be obtained, though their open sale was forbidden by the authorities, from love-philters to the wondrous fluid which, if rightly applied, would turn lead, copper, or silver to gold. Here, old women invited the passer-by to try Thracian and other spells; there, magicians stalked to and fro in painted caps and flowing, gaudy robes, most of them calling themselves priests of some god of the abyss. Men of every race and tongue that dwelt in the north of Africa, or on the shores of the Mediterranean, were packed in a noisy throng.

The greatest press was behind the houses of the men who buried the dead. Here sacrifices were offered on the altars of Serapis, Isis, and Anubis; here the sacred sistrum of Isis might be kissed; here hundreds of priests performed solemn ceremonies, and half of those who came hither for the festival of the dead collected about them. The mysteries were also performed here, beginning before midnight; and a dramatic representation might be seen of the woes of Isis, and the resurrection of her husband Osiris. But neither here, nor at the stalls, nor among the graves, where many families were feasting by torchlight and pouring libations in the sand for the souls of the dead, did Alexander expect to find his brother. Nor would Philip be attending the mysterious solemnities of any of the fraternities. He had witnessed them often enough with his friend Diodoros, who never missed the procession to Eleusis, because, as he declared, the mysteries of Demeter alone could assure a man of the immortality of the soul. The wild ceremonies of the Syrians, who maimed themselves in their mad ecstasy, repelled him as being coarse and barbarous.

As she made her way through this medley of cults, this worship of gods so different that they were in some cases hostile, but more often merged into each other, Melissa wondered to which she ought to turn in her present need. Her mother had best loved to sacrifice to Serapis and Isis. But since, in her last sickness, Melissa had offered everything she possessed to these divinities of healing, and all in vain, and since she had heard things in the Serapeum itself which even now brought a blush to her cheek, she had turned away from the great god of the Alexandrians. Though he who had offended her by such base proposals was but a priest of the lower grade—and indeed, though she knew it not, was since dead—she feared meeting him again, and had avoided the sanctuary where he officiated.

She was a thorough Alexandrian, and had been accustomed from childhood to listen to the philosophical disputations of the men about her. So she perfectly understood her brother Philip, the skeptic, when he said that he by no means denied the existence of the immortals, but that, on the other hand, he could not believe in it; that thought brought him no conviction; that man, in short, could be sure of nothing, and so could know nothing whatever of the divinity. He had even denied, on logical grounds, the goodness and omnipotence of the gods, the wisdom and fitness of the ordering of the universe, and Melissa was proud of her brother's acumen; but what appeals to the brain only, and not to the heart, can not move a woman to anything great—least of all to a decisive change of life or feeling. So the girl had remained constant to her mother's faith in some mighty powers outside herself, which guided the life of Nature and of human beings. Only she did not feel that she had found the true god, either in Serapis or Isis, and so she had sought others. Thus she had formulated a worship of ancestors, which, as she had learned from the slave-woman of her friend Ino, was not unfamiliar to the Egyptians.

In Alexandria there were altars to every god, and worship in every form. Hers, however, was not among them, for the genius of her creed was the enfranchised soul of her mother, who had cast off the burden of this perishable body. Nothing had ever come from her that was not good and lovely; and she knew that if her mother were permitted, even in some other than human form, she would never cease to watch over her with tender care.

And those initiated into the Eleusinian mysteries, as Diodoros had told her, desired the immortality of the soul, to the end that they might continue to participate in the life of those whom they had left behind. What was it that brought such multitudes at this time out to the Nekropolis, with their hands full of offerings, but the consciousness of their nearness to the dead, and of being cared for by them so long as they were not forgotten? And even if the glorified spirit of her mother were not permitted to hear her prayers, she need not therefore cease to turn to her; for it comforted her unspeakably to be with her in spirit, and to confide to her all that moved her soul. And so her mother's tomb had become her favorite place of rest. Here, if anywhere, she now hoped once more to find comfort, some happy suggestion, and perhaps some definite assistance.

She begged Alexander to take her thither, and he consented, though he was of opinion that Philip would be found in the mortuary chamber, in the presence of Korinna's portrait.

It was not easy to force their way through the thousands who had come out to the great show this night; however, most of the visitors were attracted by the mysteries far away from the Macedonian burial-ground, and there was little to disturb the silence near the fine marble monument which Alexander, to gratify his father, had erected with his first large earnings. It was hung with various garlands, and Melissa, before she prayed and anointed the stone, examined them with eye and hand.

Those which she and her father had placed there she recognized at once. That humble garland of reeds with two lotus-flowers was the gift of their old slave Argutis and his wife Dido. This beautiful wreath of choice flowers had come from the garden of a neighbor who had loved her mother well; and that splendid basketful of lovely roses, which had not been there this morning, had been placed here by Andreas, steward to the father of her young friend Diodoros, although he was of the Christian sect. And these were all. Philip had not been here then, though it was now past midnight.

For the first time in his life he had let this day pass by without a thought for their dead. How bitterly this grieved Melissa, and even added to her anxiety for him!

It was with a heavy heart that she and Alexander anointed the tombstone; and while Melissa uplifted her hands in prayer, the painter stood in silence, his eyes fixed on the ground. But no sooner had she let them fall, than he exclaimed:

"He is here, I am sure, and in the house of the embalmers. That he ordered two wreaths is perfectly certain; and if he meant one for Korinna's picture, he surely intended the other for our mother. If he has offered both to the young girl—"

"No, no!" Melissa put in. "He will bring his gift. Let us wait here a little while, and do you, too, pray to the manes of our mother. Do it to please me."

But her brother interrupted her eagerly I think of her wherever I may be; for those we truly love always live for us. Not a day passes, nor if I come in sober, not a night, when I do not see her dear face, either waking or dreaming. Of all things sacred, the thought of her is the highest; and if she had been raised to divine honors like the dead Caesars who have brought so many curses on the world—"

"Hush—don't speak so loud!" said Melissa, seriously, for men were moving to and fro among the tombs, and Roman guards kept watch over the populace.

But the rash youth went on in the same tone:

"I would worship her gladly, though I have forgotten how to pray. For who can tell here—unless he follows the herd and worships Serapis—who can tell to which god of them all he shall turn when he happens to be at his wits' end? While my mother lived, I, like you, could gladly worship and sacrifice to the immortals; but Philip has spoiled me for all that. As to the divine Caesars, every one thinks as I do. My mother would sooner have entered a pesthouse than the banqueting-hall where they feast, on Olympus. Caracalla among the gods! Why, Father Zeus cast his son Hephaistos on earth from the height of Olympus, and only broke his leg; but our Caesar accomplished a more powerful throw, for he cast his brother through the earth into the nether world—an imperial thrust—and not merely lamed him but killed him."

"Well done!" said a deep voice, interrupting the young artist. "Is that you, Alexander? Hear what new titles to fame Heron's son can find for the imperial guest who is to arrive to-morrow."

"Pray hush!" Melissa besought him, looking up at the bearded man who had laid his arm on Alexander's shoulder. It was Glaukias the sculptor, her father's tenant; for his work-room stood on the plot of ground by the garden of Hermes, which the gem-cutter had inherited from his father-in- law.

The man's bold, manly features were flushed with wine and revelry; his twinkling eyes sparkled, and the ivy-leaves still clinging to his curly hair showed that he had been one in the Dionysiac revellers; but the Greek blood which ran in his veins preserved his grace even in drunkenness. He bowed gayly to the young girl, and exclaimed to his companions:

"The youngest pearl in Alexandria's crown of beauties!" while Bion, Alexander's now gray-haired master, clapped the youth on the arm, and added: "Yes, indeed, see what the little thing has grown! Do you remember, pretty one, how you once—how many years ago, I wonder?— spotted your little white garments all over with red dots! I can see you now, your tiny finger plunged into the pot of paint, and then carefully printing off the round pattern all over the white linen. Why, the little painter has become a Hebe, a Charis, or, better still, a sweetly dreaming Psyche."

"Ay, ay!" said Glaukias again. "My worthy landlord has a charming model. He has not far to seek for a head for his best gems. His son, a Helios, or the great Macedonian whose name he bears; his daughter—you are right, Bion— the maid beloved of Eros. Now, if you can make verses, my young friend of the Muses, give us an epigram in a line or two which we may bear in mind as a compliment to our imperial visitor."

"But not here—not in the burial-ground," Melissa urged once more.

Among Glaukias's companions was Argeios, a vain and handsome young poet, with scented locks betraying him from afar, who was fain to display the promptness of his poetical powers; and, even while the elder artist was speaking, he had run Alexander's satirical remarks into the mold of rhythm. Not to save his life could he have suppressed the hastily conceived distich, or have let slip such a justifiable claim to applause. So, without heeding

Melissa's remonstrance, he flung his sky-blue mantle about him in fresh folds, and declaimed with comical emphasis:

"Down to earth did the god cast his son: but with mightier hand
    Through it, to Hades, Caesar flung his brother the dwarf."

The versifier was rewarded by a shout of laughter, and, spurred by the approval of his friends, he declared he had hit on the mode to which to sing his lines, as he did in a fine, full voice.

But there was another poet, Mentor, also of the party, and as he could not be happy under his rival's triumph, he exclaimed: "The great dyer— for you know he uses blood instead of the Tyrian shell—has nothing of Father Zeus about him that I can see, but far more of the great Alexander, whose mausoleum he is to visit to-morrow. And if you would like to know wherein the son of Severus resembles the giant of Macedon, you shall hear."

He thrummed his thyrsus as though he struck the strings of a lyre, and, having ended the dumb prelude, he sang:

"Wherein hath the knave Caracalla outdone Alexander?
    He killed a brother, the hero a friend, in his rage."

These lines, however, met with no applause; for they were not so lightly improvised as the former distich, and it was clumsy and tasteless, as well as dangerous thus to name, in connection with such a jest, the potentate at whom it was aimed. And the fears of the jovial party were only too well founded, for a tall, lean Egyptian suddenly stood among the Greeks as if he had sprung from the earth. They were sobered at once, and, like a swarm of pigeons on which a hawk swoops down, they dispersed in all directions.

Melissa beckoned to her brother to follow her; but the Egyptian intruder snatched the mantle, quick as lightning, from Alexander's shoulders, and ran off with it to the nearest pine-torch. The young man hurried after the thief, as he supposed him to be, but there the spy flung the cloak back to him, saying, in a tone of command, though not loud, for there were still many persons among the graves:

"Hands off, son of Heron, unless you want me to call the watch! I have seen your face by the light, and that is enough for this time. Now we know each other, and we shall meet again in another place!"

With these words he vanished in the darkness, and Melissa asked, in great alarm:

"In the name of all the gods, who was that?"

"Some rascally carpenter, or scribe, probably, who is in the service of the night-watch as a spy. At least those sort of folks are often built askew, as that scoundrel was," replied Alexander, lightly. But he knew the man only too well. It was Zminis, the chief of the spies to the night patrol; a man who was particularly inimical to Heron, and whose hatred included the son, by whom he had been befooled and misled in more than one wild ploy with his boon companions. This spy, whose cruelty and cunning were universally feared, might do him a serious mischief, and he therefore did not tell his sister, to whom the name of Zminis was well known, who the listener was.

He cut short all further questioning by desiring her to come at once to the mortuary hall.

"And if we do not find him there," she said, "let us go home at once; I am so frightened."

"Yes, yes," said her brother, vaguely. "If only we could meet some one you could join."

"No, we will keep together," replied Melissa, decisively; and simply assenting, with a brief "All right," the painter drew her arm through his, and they made their way through the now thinning crowd.

CHAPTER IV.

The houses of the embalmers, which earlier in the evening had shone brightly out of the darkness, now made a less splendid display. The dust kicked up by the crowd dimmed the few lamps and torches which had not by this time burned out or been extinguished, and an oppressive atmosphere of balsamic resin and spices met the brother and sister on the very threshold. The vast hall which they now entered was one of a long row of buildings of unburned bricks; but the Greeks insisted on some ornamentation of the simplest structure, if it served a public purpose, and the embalming-houses had a colonnade along their front, and their walls were covered with stucco, painted in gaudy colors, here in the Egyptian and there in the Greek taste. There were scenes from the Egyptian realm of the dead, and others from the Hellenic myths; for the painters had been enjoined to satisfy the requirements and views of visitors of every race. The chief attraction, however, this night was within; for the men whose duties were exercised on the dead had displayed the finest and best of what they had to offer to their customers.

The ancient Greek practice of burning the dead had died out under the Antonines. Of old, the objects used to deck the pyre had also been on show here; now there was nothing to be seen but what related to interment or entombment.

Side by side with the marble sarcophagus, or those of coarser stone, were wooden coffins and mummy-cases, with a place at the head for the portrait of the deceased. Vases and jars of every kind, amulets of various forms, spices and balsams in vials and boxes, little images in burned clay of the gods and of men, of which none but the Egyptians knew the allegorical meaning, stood in long rows on low wooden shelves. On the higher shelves were mummy bands and shrouds, some coarse, others of the very finest texture, wigs for the bald heads of shaven corpses, or woolen fillets, and simply or elaborately embroidered ribbons for the Greek dead.

Nothing was lacking of the various things in use for decking the corpse of an Alexandrian, whatever his race or faith.

Some mummy-cases, too, were there, ready to be packed off to other towns. The most costly were covered with fine red linen, wound about with strings of beads and gold ornaments, and with the name of the dead painted on the upper side. In a long, narrow room apart hung the portraits, waiting to be attached to the upper end of the mummy-cases of those lately deceased, and still in the hands of embalmers. Here, too, most of the lamps were out, and the upper end of the room was already dark. Only in the middle, where the best pictures were on show, the lights had been renewed.

The portraits were painted on thin panels of sycamore or of cypress, and in most of them the execution betrayed that their destiny was to be hidden in the gloom of a tomb.

Alexander's portrait of Korinna was in the middle of the gallery, in a good light, and stood out from the paintings on each side of it as a genuine emerald amid green glass. It was constantly surrounded by a crowd of the curious and connoisseurs. They pointed out the beautiful work to each other; but, though most of them acknowledged the skill of the master who had painted it, many ascribed its superiority to the magical charm of the model. One could see in those wonderfully harmonious features that Aristotle was right when he discerned beauty in order and proportion; while another declared that he found there the evidence of Plato's doctrine of the identity of the good and the beautiful—for this face was so lovely because it was the mirror of a soul which had been disembodied in the plenitude of maiden purity and virtue, unjarred by any discord; and this gave rise to a vehement discussion as to the essential nature of beauty and of virtue.

Others longed to know more about the early-dead original of this enchanting portrait. Korinna's wealthy father and his brothers were among the best-known men of the city. The elder, Timotheus, was high- priest of the Temple of Serapis; and Zeno, the younger, had set the whole world talking when he, who in his youth had been notoriously dissipated, had retired from any concern in the corn-trade carried on by his family, the greatest business of the kind in the world, perhaps, and—for this was an open secret—had been baptized.

The body of the maiden, when embalmed and graced with her portrait, was to be transported to the family tomb in the district of Arsinoe, where they had large possessions, and the gossip of the embalmer was eagerly swallowed as he expatiated on the splendor with which her liberal father proposed to escort her thither.

Alexander and Melissa had entered the portrait-gallery before the beginning of this narrative, and listened to it, standing behind several rows of gazers who were between them and the portrait.

As the speaker ceased, the little crowd broke up, and when Melissa could at last see her brother's work at her ease, she stood speechless for some time; and then she turned to the artist, and exclaimed, from the depths of her heart, "Beauty is perhaps the noblest thing in the world!"

"It is," replied Alexander, with perfect assurance. And he, bewitched once more by the spell which had held him by Korinna's couch, gazed into the dark eyes in his own picture, whose living glance his had never met, and which he nevertheless had faithfully reproduced, giving them a look of the longing of a pure soul for all that is lovely and worthy.

Melissa, an artist's daughter, as she looked at this portrait, understood what it was that had so deeply stirred her brother while he painted it; but this was not the place to tell him so. She soon tore herself away, to look about for Philip once more and then to be taken home.

Alexander, too, was seeking Philip; but, sharp as the artist's eyes were, Melissa's seemed to be keener, for, just as they were giving it up and turning to go, she pointed to a dark corner and said softly, "There he is."

And there, in fact, her brother was, sitting with two men, one very tall and the other a little man, his brow resting on his hand in the deep shadow of a sarcophagus, between the wall and a mummy-case set on end, which till now had hidden him from Alexander and Melissa.

Who could the man be who had kept the young philosopher, somewhat inaccessible in his pride of learning, so long in talk in that half-dark corner? He was not one of the learned society at the Museum; Alexander knew them all. Besides, he was not dressed like them, in the Greek fashion, but in the flowing robe of a Magian. And the stranger was a man of consequence, for he wore his splendid garment with a superior air, and as Alexander approached him he remembered having somewhere seen this tall, bearded figure, with the powerful head garnished with flowing and carefully oiled black curls. Such handsome and well-chiseled features, such fine eyes, and such a lordly, waving beard were not easily forgotten; his memory suddenly awoke and threw a light on the man as he sat in the gloom, and on the surroundings in which he had met him for the first time.

It was at the feast of Dionysus. Among a drunken crowd, which was rushing wildly along the streets, and which Alexander had joined, himself one of the wildest, this man had marched, sober and dignified as he was at this moment, in the same flowing raiment. This had provoked the feasters, who, being full of wine and of the god, would have nothing that could remind them of the serious side of life. Such sullen reserve on a day of rejoicing was an insult to the jolly giver of the fruits of the earth, and to wine itself, the care-killer; and the mad troop of artists, disguised as Silenus, satyrs, and fauns, had crowded round the stranger to compel him to join their rout and empty the wine-jar which a burly Silenus was carrying before him on his ass.

At first the man had paid no heed to the youths' light mockery; but as they grew bolder, he suddenly stood still, seized the tall faun, who was trying to force the wine-jar on him, by both arms, and, holding him firmly, fixed his grave, dark eyes on those of the youth. Alexander had not forgotten the half-comical, half-threatening incident, but what he remembered most clearly was the strange scene that followed: for, after the Magian had released his enemy, he bade him take the jar back to Silenus, and proceed on his way, like the ass, on all-fours. And the tall faun, a headstrong, irascible Lesbian, had actually obeyed the stately despot, and crept along on his hands and feet by the side of the donkey. No threats nor mockery of his companions could persuade him to rise. The high spirits of the boisterous crew were quite broken, and before they could turn on the magician he had vanished.

Alexander had afterward learned that he was Serapion, the star-gazer and thaumaturgist, whom all the spirits of heaven and earth obeyed.

When, at the time, the painter had told the story to Philip, the philosopher had laughed at him, though Alexander had reminded him that Plato even had spoken of the daimons as being the guardian spirits of men; that in Alexandria, great and small alike believed in them as a fact to be reckoned with; and that he—Philip himself—had told him that they played a prominent part in the newest systems of philosophy.

But to the skeptic nothing was sure: and if he would deny the existence of the Divinity, he naturally must disbelieve that of any beings in a sphere between the supersensual immortals and sentient human creatures. That a man, the weaker nature, could have any power over daimons, who, as having a nearer affinity to the gods, must, if they existed, be the stronger, he could refute with convincing arguments; and when he saw others nibbling whitethorn-leaves, or daubing their thresholds with pitch to preserve themselves and the house from evil spirits, he shrugged his shoulders contemptuously, though his father often did such things.

Here was Philip, deep in conversation with the man he had mocked at, and Alexander was flattered by seeing that wise and famous Serapion, in whose powers he himself believed, was talking almost humbly to his brother, as though to a superior. The magician was standing, while the philosopher, as though it were his right, remained seated.

Of what could they be conversing?

Alexander himself was anxious to be going, and only his desire to hear at any rate a few sentences of the talk of two such men detained him longer.

As he expected, it bore on Serapion's magical powers; but the bearded man spoke in a very low tone, and if the painter ventured any nearer he would be seen. He could only catch a few incoherent words, till Philip exclaimed in a louder voice: "All that is well-reasoned. But you will be able to write an enduring inscription on the shifting wave sooner than you will shake my conviction that for our spirit, such as Nature has made it, there is nothing infallible or certain."

The painter was familiar with this postulate, and was curious to hear the Magian's reply; but he could not follow his argument till he ended by saying, rather more emphatically: "You, even, do not deny the physical connection of things; but I know the power that causes it. It is the magical sympathy which displays itself more powerfully in the universe, and among human beings, than any other force."

"That is just what remains to be proved," was the reply. But as the other declared in all confidence, "And I can prove it," and was proceeding to do so, Serapion's companion, a stunted, sharp-featured little Syrian, caught sight of Alexander. The discourse was interrupted, and Alexander, pointing to Melissa, begged his brother to grant them a few minutes' speech with him. Philip, however, scarcely spared a moment for greeting his brother and sister; and when, in answer to his request that they be brief in what they had to say, they replied that a few words would not suffice, Philip was for putting them off till the morrow, as he did not choose to be disturbed just now.

At this Melissa took courage; she turned to Serapion and modestly addressed him:

"You, sir, look like a grave, kind man, and seem to have a regard for my brother. You, then, will help us, no doubt, to cure him of an illusion which troubles us. A dead girl, he says, met him, and he touched her hand."

"And do you, sweet child, think that impossible?" the Magian asked with gentle gravity. "Have the thousands who bring not merely fruit and wine and money for their dead, but who even burn a black sheep for them—you, perhaps, have done the same—have they, I ask, done this so long in vain? I can not believe it. Nay, I know from the ghosts themselves that this gives them pleasure; so they must have the organs of sense."

"That we may rejoice departed souls by food and drink," said Melissa, eagerly, "and that daimons at times mingle with the living, every one of course, believes; but who ever heard that warm blood stirred in them? And how can it be possible that they should remunerate a service with money, which certainly was not coined in their airy realm, but in the mint here?"

"Not too fast, fair maid," replied the Magian, raising a warning hand. "There is no form which these intermediate beings can not assume. They have the control of all and everything which mortals may use, so the soul of Korinna revisiting these scenes may quite well have paid the ferryman with an obolus."

"Then you know of it?" asked Melissa in surprise; but the Magian broke in, saying:

"Few such things remain hidden from him who knows, not even the smallest, if he strives after such knowledge."

As he spoke he gave the girl such a look as made her eyelids fall, and he went on with greater warmth: "There would be fewer tears shed by death- beds, my child, if we could but show the world the means by which the initiated hold converse with the souls of the dead."

Melissa shook her pretty head sadly, and the Magian kindly stroked her waving hair; then, looking her straight in the eyes, he said: "The dead live. What once has been can never cease to be, any more than out of nothing can anything come. It is so simple; and so, too, are the workings of magic, which amaze you so much. What you call magic, when I practice it, Eros, the great god of love, has wrought a thousand times in your breast. When your heart leaps at your brother's caress, when the god's arrow pierces you, and the glance of a lover fills you with gladness, when the sweet harmonies of fine music wrap your soul above this earth, or the wail of a child moves you to compassion, you have felt the magic power stirring in your own soul. You feel it when some mysterious power, without any will of your own, prompts you to some act, be it what it may. And, besides all this, if a leaf flutters off the table without being touched by any visible hand, you do not doubt that a draught of air, which you can neither hear nor see, has swept through the room. If at noon the world is suddenly darkened, you know, without looking up at the sky, that it is overcast by a cloud. In the very same way you can feel the nearness of a soul that was dear to you without being able to see it. All that is necessary is to strengthen the faculty which knows its presence, and give it the proper training, and then you will see and hear them. The Magians have the key which unlocks the door of the world of spirits to the human senses. Your noble brother, in whom the claims of the spirit have long since triumphed over those of sense, has found this key without seeking it, since he has been permitted to see Korinna's soul. And if he follows a competent guide he will see her again."

"But why? What good will it do him?" asked Melissa, with a reproachful and anxious look at the man whose influence, as she divined would be pernicious to her brother, in spite of his knowledge. The Magian gave a compassionate shrug, and in the look he cast at the philosopher, the question was legible, "What have such as these to do with the highest things?"

Philip nodded in impatient assent, and, without paying any further heed to his brother and sister, besought his friend to give him the proofs of the theory that the physical causation of things is weaker than the sympathy which connects them. Melissa knew full well that any attempt now to separate Philip from Serapion would be futile; however, she would not leave the last chance untried, and asked him gravely whether he had forgotten his mother's tomb.

He hastily assured her that he fully intended to visit it presently. Fruit and fragrant oil could be had here at any hour of the night.

"And your two wreaths?" she said, in mild reproach, for she had observed them both below the portrait of Korinna.

"I had another use for them," he said, evasively; and then he added, apologetically: "You have brought flowers enough, I know. If I can find time, I will go to-morrow to see my father." He nodded to them both, turned to the Magian, and went on eagerly:

"Then that magical sympathy—"

They did not wait to hear the discussion; Alexander signed to his sister to follow him.

He, too, knew that his brother's ear was deaf now to anything he could say. What Serapion had said had riveted even his attention, and the question whether it might indeed be vouchsafed to living mortals to see the souls of the departed, and hear their voices, exercised his mind so greatly that he could not forbear asking his sister's opinion on such matters.

But Melissa's good sense had felt that there was something not quite sound in the Magian's argument—nor did she conceal her conviction that Philip, who was always hard to convince, had accepted Serapion's views, not because he yielded to the weight of his reasons, but because he—and Alexander, too, for that matter—hoped by his mediation to see the beautiful Korinna again.

This the artist admitted; but when he jested of the danger of a jealous quarrel between him and his brother, for the sake of a dead girl, there was something hard in his tone, and very unlike him, which Melissa did not like.

They breathed more freely as they got out into the open air, and her efforts to change the subject of their conversation were happily seconded; for at the door they met the family of their neighbor Skopas, the owner of a stone-quarry, whose grave-plot adjoined theirs, and Melissa was happy again as she heard her brother laughing as gayly as ever with Skopas's pretty daughter. The mania had not taken such deep hold of the light-hearted young painter as of Philip, the poring and gloomy philosopher; and she was glad as she heard her friend Ino call Alexander a faithless butterfly, while her sister Helena declared that he was a godless scoffer.

———————

Milton Keynes UK
Ingram Content Group UK Ltd.
UKHW041158040324
438885UK00007B/485